It's Haircut ✂ Time!

by Michele Griffin

Sensory World
A proud imprint of   Future Horizons

It's Haircut Time!

All marketing and publishing rights guaranteed to and reserved by:

1010 N. Davis Drive
Arlington, Texas 76012
(877) 775-8968
(682) 558-8941
(682) 558-8945 (fax)

E-mail: info@sensoryworld.com
www.sensoryworld.com

Cover and Interior Layout by Cindy Williams

Printed in Canada

ISBN 13: 978-1-935567-33-2

For all those who have sweated
and suffered over a haircut......including BG and JB!

OH DEAR!

It's here!

The day...

Moan and groan,

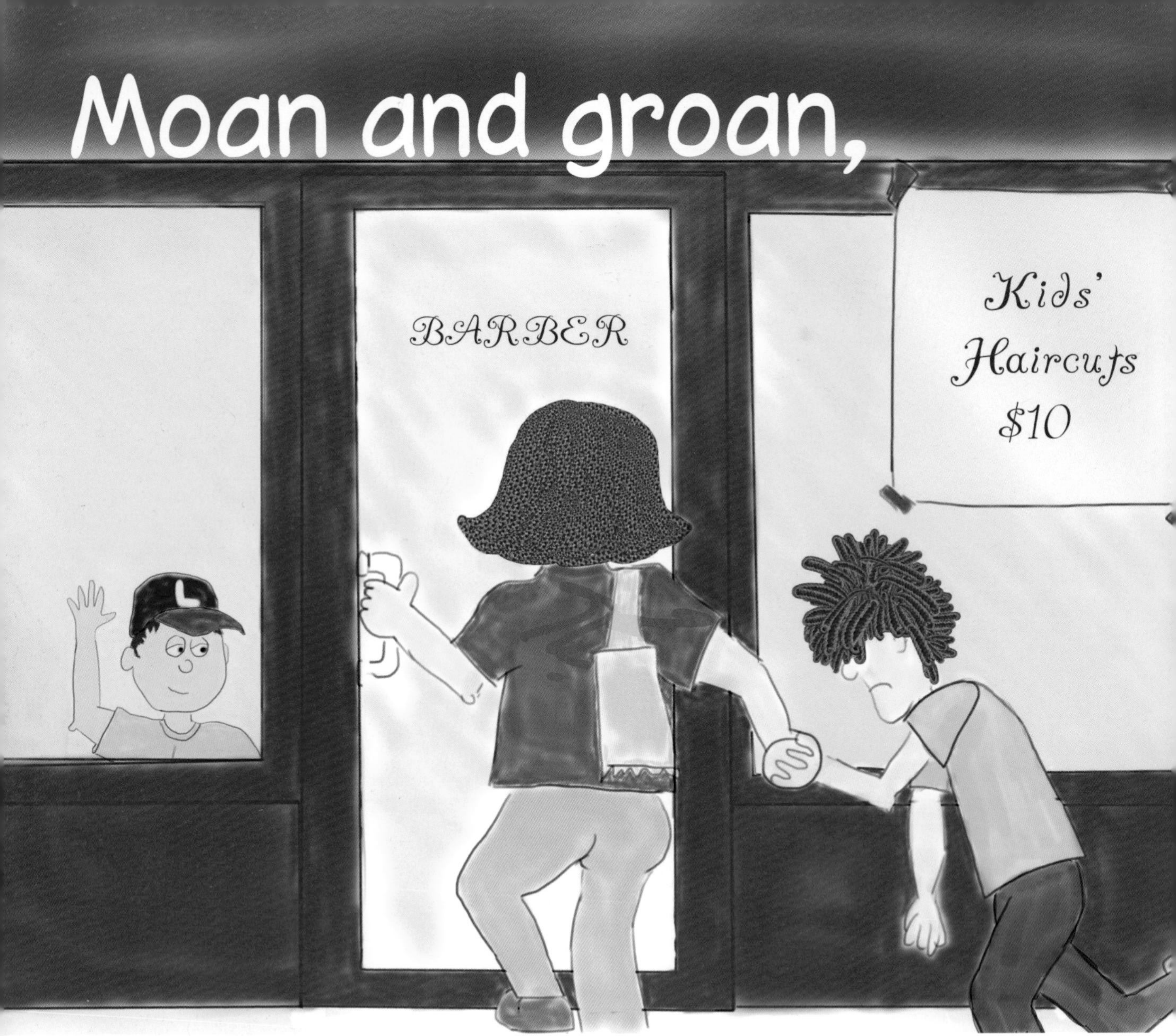

I feel so alone.

The chair is so high,

I believe I might die.

Next the cold, slippery cape does not feel so great.

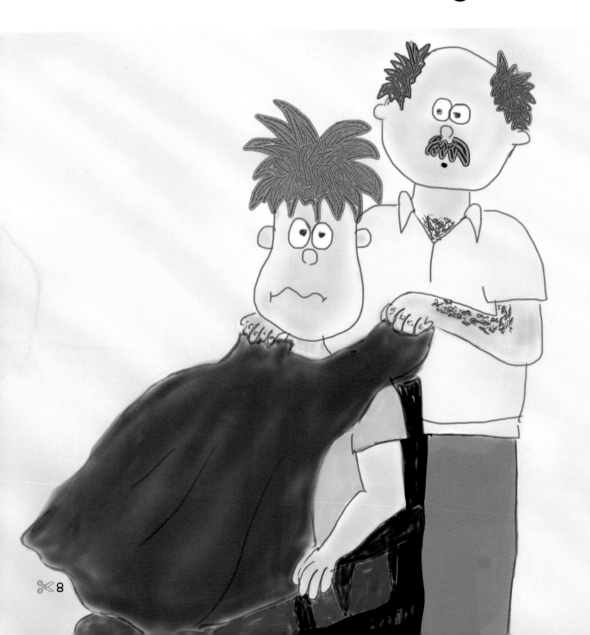

Now the water spray, I bet . . . .
My face will get wet!

NO WAY!

NOT TODAY!

Very quickly?

Grrr . . . well . . . . OK.

Stop touching my head!

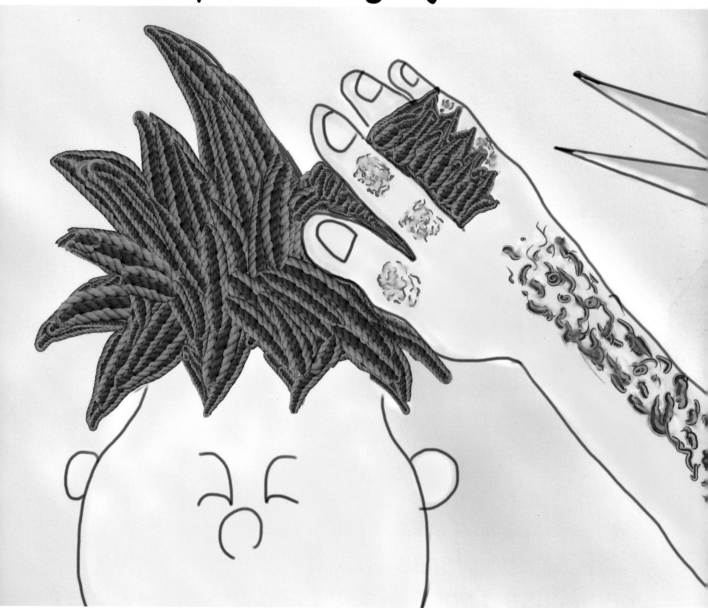

Take me back to bed!

13

Snip! Snap! Hair in my lap!

Bits and pieces falling here and there,
once just a part of me . . . don't they care?

The tickling has started at the tip of my nose,

a terrible feeling right down to my toes!

If I had my way, I'd never cut a hair.
I'd keep it long and lush with curls everywhere!

All of this is really getting to me . . .
Take a deep breath . . . count 1, 2, 3.

17 ✂

What, Mom? Think of happy things?
To keep my mind off the
snips and drips and horrid things?

Well, here I go . . . happy things that I know . . .

Picking flowers and smelling the
scent with my nose.

Swimming with dolphins
is easy to do with my eyes closed.

A huge chocolate bar, only for me.

Thinking happy thoughts makes me feel free!

Dancing outside with my friends,

Staying up late and watching a movie to the end!

At the zoo watching monkeys and leopards with spots.

Licking cherry-flavored lollipops!

Lollipop? Huh? What? For me?

You are finished with my haircut?

Another great Sensory World title by Michele!

Picky, Picky Pete

A Boy and His Sensory Challenges

by Michele Griffin

CREATIVE TOY AWARDS
Creative Child Magazine
2010
BOOK
of the
Year Award
www.creativechild.com

Other Children's Books

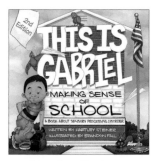

Hartley Steiner

Jennie Harding

Beverly Bishop

Marla Roth-Fisch

Carol Gray

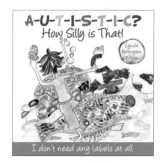

Carol Kranowitz

Lynda Farrington Wilson

All of these titles and more are at
www.sensoryworld.com

Additional Resources

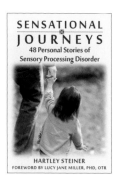

Hartley Steiner

Doreit Bialer
& Lucy Miller

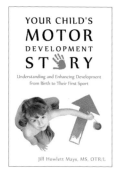

Jill Mays

Rebecca Moyes

David & Kathy Jereb

Aubrey Lande, Bob
Wiz, & Lois Hickman

Beth Aune, Beth Burt,
& Peter Gennaro

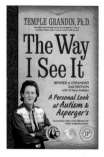

Temple Grandin

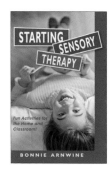

Bonnie Arnwine

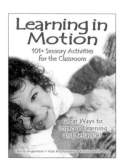

Patricia Angermeier, Joan
Kryzanowski, & Kristina Keller Moir

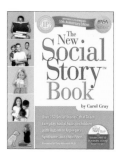

Carol Gray

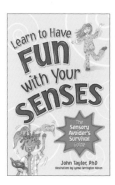

John Taylor

Carol Kranowitz

Find these and other great resources
at www.sensoryworld.com

These catalog companies can provide more ideas and products for kids with special needs.

School Speciality
(888) 388-3224
www.schoolspecialtyonline.net

FlagHouse Sensory Solution
(800) 793-7900
www.FlagHouse.com

Henry Occupational Therapy Services, Inc.
(623) 882-8812
www.ateachabout.com

Therapro, Inc.
(800) 257-5376
www.theraproducts.com